Very little Red Riding Hood

Teresa Heapy & Sue Heap

HOUGHTON MIFFLIN HARCOURT   Boston New York

For Ella. —T.H.

For all librarians, especially Judith,
plus Liz, Laura, and Ceri. —S.H.

Originally published in Great Britain by
David Fickling Books, a division of Random House
Children's Publishers UK, 2013

Text copyright © 2014 by Teresa Heapy
Illustrations copyright © 2014 by Sue Heap

www.hmhco.com

The text of this book is set in OPTI Adminster Book.
The illustrations are watercolor and ink.

ISBN 978-0-544-28000-7

Manufactured in China
TOP 10 9 8 7 6 5 4 3 2 1
4500456941

Very Little Red Riding Hood was going to
her Grandmama's for a sleepover.

"I go see Gramma with cakes,"
      said **Very** <small>Little</small> Red Riding Hood.

"Yes, my love, I know," said her Mummy.

"Off you go.
Be gentle with
Grandmama.
And don't break
anything!"

"Bye bye, my
Mummy!" said
Very Little Red
Riding Hood.

So **Very** Little Red Riding Hood set off for Grandmama's house.

She hadn't gotten very far when she met a Wolf.

"**A Foxie!**" said **Very** Little Red Riding Hood.

She gave him a **big** hug.

"Aren't you scared?" asked the Wolf.

"I **not** scared!
I Very Little Red Riding Hood,
that's what I am!"
said
Very
Little
Red Riding
Hood.

"I go see Gramma with cakes,"
said Very Little Red Riding Hood.
"Oh, good," said the Wolf.
"Can I have one?"

"**No!**" said
Very Little
Red Riding Hood.

"No touch my cakes!"

The Wolf tried again.
"Can I come too?"

"NO!" shouted Very Little
Red Riding Hood.

"Go 'WAY!"

The Wolf tried once more.

"Look at these lovely flowers," he said. "We could pick some for your Grandmama."

"NOOO!"

screamed Very Little Red Riding Hood.

Not LELLO flowers. RED!

So they picked some red flowers.

"Come on, Foxie," said
Very Little Red Riding Hood.
"We go this way!
Chase me!"

So the Wolf had to

chase **Very** Little Red Riding Hood

all the way

to Grandmama's house.

Very Little Red Riding Hood knocked on Grandmama's door. "I come see you, Gramma. Look! Cakes!" she said.

"Well, it's lovely to see you, dear," said Grandmama.

And then . . .

"HELP!
There's a Wolf
on the doorstep!"

"I come for sleepover,"
said **Very** Little
Red Riding Hood, firmly.

"I got my bag,

and Red Teddy,

and my cups,

and my blanket.

Foxie, d'you want
a cup of tea?"

"*He* **can't** come in!" said Grandmama.
"Oh, Gramma, it's only Foxie,"
said **Very** Little
Red Riding Hood.

So the Wolf came in
and took a cup of tea from
Very Little Red Riding Hood.

They all had a cup of tea.

Then they played
hide-and-seek.

Then they
did dancing.

Then they did drawing.

Then they had another cup of tea.

And another.

The Wolf and Grandmama were getting quite tired.

But then **Very** <small>Little</small> Red Riding Hood remembered something.

Or somebody.

**"I don't know where is
my Mummy,"**
said **Very** <small>Little</small> Red Riding Hood.

"I want my Mummy!"

Very Little Red Riding Hood
was very upset.

Grandmama tried
a story.

She tried a hug.

She tried Red Teddy.

"Mr. Wolf, we're in trouble," she said.

"Can you help?"

So the Wolf tried.

"Oh, what big, wet eyes you have," he said.

"Oh, what a **big,** snotty nose you have," he said.

And then,

"Oh, what a **big, red MOUTH** you have," said the Wolf.

"And ..."

"I'm

going to . . .

give you a great
big tickle!"

So the Wolf tickled
Very Little Red Riding Hood.

He tickled her arms, her ribs, and her toes.
He tickled her chin, her ears, and her nose.

Very Little Red Riding Hood stopped crying.

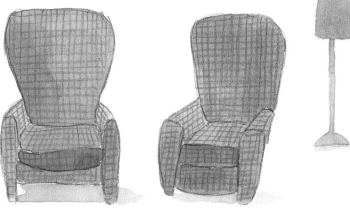

She laughed.

She laughed and laughed and laughed.

And then she fell asleep.

And they all slept happily ever after.